THE BABA YAGA TREE SHORT TALL STORIES

JULIE FEARN

Copyright © 2024 by Julie Fearn

The right of Julie Fearn to be identified as the author of this work has been asserted by her in accordance with the Copyright, Designs and Patents Act 1988.

All rights reserved. No part of this publication may be reproduced, distributed, or transmitted in any form or by any means, including photocopying, recording, or other electronic or mechanical methods, without the prior written permission of the author, except in the case of brief quotations embodied in critical reviews and certain other noncommercial uses permitted by copyright law.

Cover Image by Michael Rollins.

Contents

1. CORONATION DEVIL   1
2. CRAFTY HOUSE   7
3. THE SMUG BASTARD   18
4. KIRKSTONE PASS   23
5. COCKTAILS WITH MARIE, 1994   29
6. THE BABA YAGA TREE   34
7. FACE OFF   42
8. WILD NIGHT   47
9. AREA 523   53
10. HEY JOE   56
11. THE LIGHTHOUSE   62

12.	CEDRIC'S CHRISTMAS	67
13.	THE SUITCASE OF SECRETS	70
14.	ABOUT JULIE FEARN	87

CORONATION DEVIL

Purple-faced Stanley talked incessantly. I had to ask him to be quiet during the oath bit because it was history in the making. I didn't actually care, but at least I wasn't home alone. The reds and golds of the coronation extravaganza swirled as we watched, guzzling Prosecco, Malbec, and Variety sandwiches from M&S. The spring sun flowed through the nets and created a shimmery haze. Cocooned in Betty's world of china and brass, I felt nostalgic for the comfort of family and bygone days. Afterwards, I staggered home along the sun-blanched street of bungalows as Union Jacks snapped in the wind. A remark of Stanley's had unsettled me, but what's the point of challenging strangers? I had no plans to hook up with him and Betty again.

I had to pass Stanley's and Betty's bungalows every day to walk my dog. They lived next to one another and were constantly popping in and out of each other's houses. I thought it was sweet, and secretly envied them. No one popped into my house these days because, after my last accident, supine in bed with a leg encased in purple plaster, I'd decided to give up my drinking pals and the pub sessions that resulted in excruciating angst and puzzling bruises. The weird group camaraderie of *being able to take your drink* disturbed me.

'Cooee!' Betty sprang from her doorway using the pensioner wall handles and limped up the drive to greet Molly and me.

'That was fun the other day.' A smile exposed her yellow teeth as she eagerly awaited a positive reply. I answered almost truthfully. 'Yes, it was enjoyable. Thanks for inviting me.'

'Would Molly like some biscuits?'

Before I could answer, Betty spun back to fetch some.

Molly wagged her tail and snuffled into Betty's cream slacks after gobbling the biscuits. Stanley slipped from behind his hedge and bent to pat Molly. 'Hello, boy.'

'She's a girl. Her name's Molly.'

I hoped I didn't sound harsh.

Stanley breathed fumes into Molly's face, and she backed away.

'We should do it again,' Betty called from her gate as I tugged Molly from the driveway.

'Yes,' I said, not meaning it.

Summer arrived early. The cavernous blue sky blasted the sun's heat down daily. The earth frizzled before the flowers opened their skirts, and the young grass shrank back. My birthday was soon. Its approach oppressed me. Two friends would join me on the day. But that was tomorrow. Today, the sunlight bounced on my patio as the bees wobbled on the lavender. Fuck it! I didn't want to be alone on such a glorious day.

Stanley opened his door before I knocked. In the dark of the doorway, his face appeared more navy than purple. I tugged at Molly's lead and said, 'Molly would like you and Betty to come for a drink in our garden.' I could feel the colour creeping over my face.

Effervescent with wine when my friend left early on my birthday, I phoned Stanley. My senses were tamped down. We agreed to meet up soon for another drinks and snacks affair. *Why not!* I thought as I poured myself another wine that twinkled in the crystal glass.

··········

Sitting on Betty's floral sofa, my bare toes dug into her fluffy rug, I felt happy. Stanley asked me if I liked the Eagles.

'Yes, of course.' It was true. I was young in the 1970s.

'What other kinds of music do you like?' Betty asked me, displaying her perfect yellow teeth in a rictus smile.

'I like all types. My taste's eclectic.'

'But who's your favourite singer?'

'I don't do favourites.'

Betty shuffled on her armchair. 'I like Fleetwood Mac.'

Pretty impressive for eighty, I thought.

She wanted to pin my tastes down, so I said, 'Van Morrison's one of my favourite singers.'

'The Eagles are the best group in the world,' said Stanley, and got up to play *The Best of The Eagles* CD. He bent over the player with his hairy arms and said, '*She* didn't know who Fleetwood Mac was until I told her.'

Betty smiled at me. 'My husband used to like James Last and His Orchestra.'

I nodded and swigged my Prosecco as Molly snoozed by my feet.

And so, it went on, dropping in and out for a drink and chat about Fleetwood Mac and the Eagles.

·············

Call me clumsy if you like, but another fall grounded me, a broken ankle this time. Stanley and Betty leapt at the chance to walk Molly daily. They were kind, and there was no one else unless I paid some dog-walker, who would tether Molly to a large group of dogs and drag them through the park in a snarling pack from which parents and children would shrink.

Stanley liked the Teatime Walk best and began bringing two bottles of wine for a *cheeky* post-walk drink. Red for him, white for me and Betty, who only ever drank one small glass as she sat on my sofa, gazing at Stanley as he rambled about the Eagles.

Stanley began to bring a bottle of red for *after* the morning walks. With his boyish smile, he insisted that the sun was past the yardarm. Betty sipped gingerly, and I said, 'Not for me, thanks.'

He would ask after three-quarters of the bottle had slid down his throat, 'Is it okay if I play *Hotel California*?'

He'd riffled my music collection on his first visit and pounced on his two favourites.

'Actually, I'd like to have a nap soon.' I glanced at Betty, who was raptured in his presence.

· · · • · · • · · · ·

That evening, they arrived with a DVD and more bottles.

'We can all watch a film,' Betty said brightly as she settled into the sofa.

As Stanley bent to slap the DVD into the gaping maw of the tray, he said, 'This is a great film, at the end...'

But I stopped him.

'Don't spoil it for us, Stanley. Betty hasn't seen it, and I've forgotten.'

But Stanley stood back from the player, one hand on his jutting hip, the other fidgeting for something not there.

'At the end,' he began again.

I looked at Betty for support, but she gazed adoringly at Stanley.

Stanley had revealed the film's ending and added more, so he suggested we listen to the Eagles.

'I've got loads of music, Stanley,' I said. 'Why don't you choose something different?'

He stumbled towards the shelf and noisily pulled CDs in and out to inspect them.

'I've never heard of them,' he said, now and then, 'or them,' as he clattered through my collection.

Betty sat silently, waiting for Stanley to choose the music, just like her dead husband had. Eventually, he yanked something out and turned towards me.

'What's this weird stuff then?'

'It's a collection of alternative country, you know, the Handsome Family...'

Stanley stared hard at me.

Behind him, the evening sun illuminated his silhouette through the French doors. Stanley's features were obscured, and his face was a darkened blur. The long black hairs on his lower arms were raised in curls with dust motes floating off like tiny fires. He resembled the Devil. His claw hands unfurled at his sides. I didn't want to hear any more Eagles or Fleetwood Mac. I didn't want to drink with an alcoholic who leeched friendship, and filled my glass to overflowing and shrugged when I'd mentioned, after one of their visits, that I'd fallen over and banged my head on the skirting board, which could have been so much worse. I could have snapped my neck and been paralysed or, like Marianne Faithfull, crashed down drunk and shattered her jaw on the floor of her New York apartment. I had to escape from losers needing to start swigging early and continue until late, until insensate, who saw it as *a bit of fun*, something not for weaklings. I wanted to push Stanley out of my door, for him to fall, his skull to crack wide open and pour out thick red blood like my hate for him. I glanced to check for cloven hooves. He was in his beige moccasin slippers. As I stared at Stanley, he came back into view. His purple face emerged from the backlight. His hands trembled as those of alcoholics do. I saw his weakness and felt mine. I needed to run away. But I couldn't, not with my injury.

'Stanley,' I said. 'Shut up and pour me a drink.'

CRAFTY HOUSE

I'm fearful.

The couple burst from their red Porsche to judge the front driveway, frown at the blown daffodils and rusted gate.

'It needs a lick of paint,' Sasha says to Gerry, shoving the gate shut.

The estate agent remarks, 'This is a 1920s Arts and Crafts house, with original features throughout.'

I feel relieved. That's my unique selling point, my heart and soul.

'Very sought after.' He smiles at them, jingling the keys.

In they come. I swallow all three into my panelled hallway. Resist burping.

'Oohs' and 'aahs' reverberate in the house's emptiness. They skip upstairs. The centrepiece of the master bedroom is a mahogany fire surround, floral and fluted, hand-carved in the early twentieth century. The fire's blaze becomes the heart of the room in winter. The couple rush inside, and Sasha squeezes Gerry's arm. 'Oh, my God! Look at that massive garden!'

She gestures towards the window, gold bracelets jangling. Below, the Italianate garden shimmers in the sunlight. At its centre, a lily pond is sheltered by cypresses. A topiary-lined path curves away to a modest fountain, where an obelisk rises to the heavens.

'Are there any building restrictions?' Sasha enquires.

The estate agent flicks through his screen. 'Nope.'

'We're thinking open-plan, with living and working areas combined, divided by an indoor pool,' Gerry adds.

Everything prickles for me. They can't be serious.

Sasha beams at the agent.

'Cool,' he says.

'The sale should be speedy,' he says later, swinging open their car door. 'The owner died, and her family want closure.'

·········

Now, the sign outside reads *Sold (subject to contract)*. When the builders arrive, a purple-faced man raps the oak panels with his dirty knuckles. 'We'll rip this out,' he says.

His chum sucks on a soggy roll-up in the hallway. 'Car boot it.'

Car boot? I don't think so, matey. Here I come.

Chum's tobacco tin slowly vibrates to the edge of the windowsill.

Whoops!

His tobacco splashes across the golden oak parquet floor.

'Shit!' He scrambles on his skinny knees to collect it.

Now they clump round to peer and poke, scratching their heads. 'Where should the pool go? What the...?'

Purple-face can't finish because he stumbles sideways. The house sways like a ship. It creaks and undulates. 'This is freaky,' he says.

What fun.

They whizz off in their yellow van.

Wimps.

Later in the week, a surveyor arrives loaded with instruments. His laser pierces the house's William Morris wallpaper and beeps. He waits for Sasha to pick up her phone.

'There's no evidence of subsidence,' he says. 'The builders must have been imagining things.'

The surveyor struts towards the window and peers out. 'No old mines in the area either.' He advises her, 'It's a lucrative investment. Go ahead.'

I'm afraid I have to disagree.

Soon, an electrician examines the wiring. He pulls raggedy strands from a small aperture in the wall.

'What the devil..?'

I don't let him finish.

Bang!

The electrician jolts backwards and drops to the floor. Smoke puffs out from the cavity. Surprised, he clutches the ruptured wires in one hand.

Let go, why don't you?

The builders are back, scrutinising the architect's plans. Purple-face hunkers down to locate the floor joists.

Superficial damage is acceptable at times.

Boom! Plaster plummets from the ceiling and crashes into splinters across the floor.

'I'm packing it in,' the builder tells Sasha as he lets her in later. 'It's not bloody safe.'

But, in September, the *Sold* sign is torn down.

I'm astonished.

A van rumbles down the driveway and crunches into the old oak tree. The squirrels flee in all directions, homeless.

'It's okay,' Sasha says, 'it has to go anyway. It's blocking the light.'

No! I say to myself. You have to go.

The architect nods as Sasha outlines her plans for an observatory above the pool.

'Planning permission might be a problem.' He smiles at her.

Sasha does not smile back.

'You might need to scale it down a little.'

'This is our forever house,' she simpers, twirling her blond hair around pointed green fingernails.

'Renovations do need to be in sympathy with the property.' The architect's phone bleeps. He answers it and looks away, relieved.

'I'll take your plans and see what I can come up with.'

He turns and falters, resting one arm on the walnut bannister. 'Out of interest,' he says, his cheeks colouring, 'why did you choose this house?'

'We didn't buy the house,' Sasha laughs, 'we bought the space.'

Tonight, I am going to make her regret this.

'That fireplace is a total monstrosity,' Sasha says, as she slides into the super-king-size bed. 'Have you even heard of William Morris?' She scratches her head, absently.

Gerry pulls the sash window up and down. 'Sort of,' he says. He turns to her. 'You know these are quite funky,' he adds.

'Hideous!' Sasha yanks open her Apple Mac. 'They remind me of draughty student lets.' She shivers exaggeratedly.

'Oh, poor little poor girl,' Gerry says.

They've fallen asleep. Abandoned screens flicker on each side of the bed. The moon is full, and a sliver of beam slips through the gap in the curtains. They snuffle, turn, and Sasha thrusts out her fake tan arm.

I begin with the door.

The door opens and then closes, opens and closes again and again. Sasha wakes first.

'Gerry, is that you?'

He grunts and rolls over.

I turn my attention to the walls.

The walls bend out slightly, bend back in, and bend out again, creaking and groaning.

Repeat when necessary.

Plaster is dislodged from the bowed walls.

Oops! Sorry about the mess, little ones.

Sasha grabs the lamp with one hand and shakes Gerry with the other.

'Wake up!'

He sits up and stares at the shape-shifting walls. 'Am I seeing things?'

'No!' Sasha opens her mouth, but the words freeze in her throat.

Perhaps a little more is needed.

The floor rumbles and the bed judders. Sasha scrambles out first. Her foot tangles in the duvet and she falls forward.

'Oh, God!' Sasha grabs Gerry's arm for stability.

'We have to get out,' she says. 'It's an earthquake!'

They scramble downstairs, yank on coats, stumble into shoes and rush outdoors. The moon shines as they tremble on the damp lawn, tapping their phone screens.

The next morning, Gerry stares out of the kitchen window as starlings gather on the fence - the boot boys of the bird world.

'I hate those bloody things.' Sasha pulls a face. 'When they clatter about on the roof, it sounds like they're inside.'

Gerry turns to Sasha in a flash of inspiration.

'Maybe that's it. What if there's an infestation here?'

Sasha halts her facial exercise and puts down the mirror.

'Oh, God. Like what, for example?'

'Mice maybe - I don't know.'

I see this worries her.

'I'll make some calls, shall I?' Sasha waggles her pink phone. Gerry dances over. 'Yeah, do.' He picks up her hand and thumbs the delicate butterfly wrist tattoo. 'We've been so wrapped up in the house. Let's take some time out.'

'We can't just run off abroad.' Sasha stiffens.

'Who said abroad, missy? What about the Lakes for a weekend?' He bends to kiss the top of her head.

'I'll call you this afternoon.' Sasha looks up at him, her face serious. 'I really want this to work.'

'What?' Gerry steps back for a second.

'The house, silly, I mean the house.'

'Yeah, of course. Not enough sleep,' Gerry says, squeezing Sasha's hand and heading to the door. 'Love you to the moon and back.'

Oh, my god!

Later, the Rentokil man strolls up to the house, blabbing into his mobile. He flicks his cigarette onto the clean path.

Philistine!

It takes him thirty-five minutes to examine the loft for signs of rodent life.

'Nothing there,' he tells Sasha, descending.

Tut tut!

She stands with her arms crossed at the foot of the ladder and suggests he scrabble underneath the stair cupboard.

It's time to turn up the volume.

The cupboard door slams. The lock jams as Rentokil frantically rattles it.

'Hey!' he shouts. 'Open up! Let me out!'

Sasha tugs at the door for ten minutes. Red-faced and sweaty, she phones Gerry.

Rentokil continues to bang and yell.

Maybe he's claustrophobic. Anyway, it's become tiresome, so I let him go.

Thwang!

The door opens. He staggers forward and beats the cobwebs from his overalls. He turns to Sasha to say, 'You could have...' just as the wrought iron chandelier thumps down on his head. Rentokil wobbles for a moment before collapsing.

Oh dear! Blood splatter on my parquet floor. Now, I release the rodents.

The rats move like waves across the floor. Some branch off to scrabble upstairs. Sasha screams, jumps over Rentokil and runs.

Before they go to sleep that night, Sasha says, 'we might need some expert help.'

'Such as?'

'Well, it sounds crazy, but like an exorcist, maybe.'

'No way,' Gerry says. 'You've got to be kidding?'

'I'm not. What if it's haunted...'

Gerry pats Sasha's bare shoulder. 'Let's discuss it tomorrow.'

Feel free to discuss all you want. I'm not going anywhere.

··········

A digger ripping up the back garden disturbs the quiet of the morning. The lanky driver, wearing red headphones, sings along as his machine bumps and crashes through the innocent shrubs to churn up the lawn. His mate yanks a chainsaw and it screams into action.

Sasha stands beside the mayhem, talking animatedly with the architect. The trees fall like wounded soldiers. Sasha puts on her reading glasses, points at the plans, and smiles. She flashes the digger man a thumbs up and returns inside to throw brunch together.

'I can't wait to get rid of those ghastly doors,' Sasha says as she smashes avocado into a hot wrap. 'I want sliding glass panels, floor to ceiling.'

'What darling wants, darling gets.' Gerry picks up an apple and crunches into it.

'Ugh! It's off,' he spits it out. 'But we have to keep some supporting walls.'

....

The siren wails as the ambulance speeds off to the hospital. Sasha and Gerry sit in astonished silence, an empty bottle of Sancerre between them. Gerry's found some cigarettes, and they both puff away. Eventually, Sasha speaks. 'Do you think he'll lose his leg?'

Gerry stands up. 'I've been thinking, maybe it's time for your exorcist.'

Bring it on.

A wafer-thin man floats into the room. His name is Frederick, and he's East European. The three of them huddle around the table in the dining room. Light falls from the ceiling, transforming Frederick's silver hair into a shimmering halo. He glances from one to the other and looks down, studying his long-fingered hands.

'I don't know how to say this.' His eyes are luminous.

'Yes?' They chime together, leaning in.

'There's no spirit here,' he shrugs. 'It's not a ghost.'

'Can't you sense *anything* at all?' Sasha looks about to cry.

His expression shifts. Frederick spreads his pale fingers out on the table, scrutinises the bewildered couple for a while, closes his eyes, and tunes into something.

I notice his skin is near-translucent.

'This is going to sound odd.' Frederick opens his eyes and examines the couple intently for a sign of permission.

'Go on,' Gerry says. His arm slowly circles Sasha's shoulders.

'You said you're making lots of changes to this house.'

They nod.

'Some houses,' Frederick says, 'in my experience, don't like change.'

Gerry laughs first. Then, a dark shadow crosses his face. He releases Sasha and leans over the table.

'How much are we paying you for this shit?'

Frederick rises slowly and lifts his white coat from the chair. 'It's free,' he says and quietly leaves the room.

Thank you, Frederick, I say. A kindred spirit of sorts.

The next day, Gerry dials Frederick's number. He'd slept on things and has some questions to run by him.

'The number you have dialled has not been recognised,' says the automated voice.

He calls again and again. 'How strange.'

Eventually, Gerry shouts upstairs, 'Sasha, we need to talk.'

·········

The *For Sale* sign has been planted in the recuperating lawn.

I'm so pleased.

A beat-up orange camper van rattles up the drive and cranks to a stop. The driver's door swings open to reveal a grinning woman, whose wild red hair spills from a colourful bandeau. She jumps down onto the gravel in a satisfying crunch. A second later, a springer spaniel bounces out. He barks and circles her excitedly.

'This house has William Morris wallpaper,' she says to the dog as she ruffles his ears. A blond boy of about six clambers down.

Glancing around, he smiles and runs towards the door, chased by his dog.

I know they will prefer me as I am. At last, I can rest.

Welcome, I whisper.

THE SMUG BASTARD

When I finally found his cliché, I let out a cry of joy. The librarian's face stiffened. Four months had passed since I heard that radio interview, four gruelling months spent interrogating his novels for the presence of a cliché.

'Cliché is our enemy,' Mr Big Wig writer had smugly intoned to the fawning presenter of the *Best Writers of The Decade* radio programme. Then came, 'Giselle plunged into the foaming sea. Her lithe, sun-kissed body shimmered like a baby seal's.'

He was reading from my rejected manuscript, as an example of clichéd writing. How dare he? So, I made it my mission to search his novels for the enemy's presence. A boring task, admittedly. Trawling through his work, I found that, remarkably, none of his characters were likeable. Action scenes were entirely absent. Moreover, uncovering the plots was fiendish. Even worse, his stories started at the end or in the middle. But, praise be to God, my mission was accomplished at last. Later that day, I phoned Pam to share the intelligence.

'It might be better if you concentrate on finishing your new novel, Geoffrey.'

'I can't. Not until I've unmasked that fraud.'

'But, remember, our writing tutor said to keep focussed.'

'I am focussed,' I told her and decided on my next manoeuvre then and there: I would write a letter to The Times, exposing him as a poser.

May 10, 2013

Sir,

Apropos of Tom Maye's interview on Radio 4's The Write Word, aired on January 9th 2013, I would make the following observation. Mr Maye claims he leads the war against the evils of poor writing. He proclaims he does this by executing the cliché with his firing squad of modern novels. This is an admirable aspiration, but I am sorry to say that he is hoisted by his own petard. On reading his novel, 'Mote', I was surprised to find this sentence: 'I strode across her writhing body.' Is this not the deployment of cliché? Therefore, in his mission to seek and destroy the cliché, I declare he has lost his battle.

Yours faithfully,

Geoffrey Barnet, Sergeant (Ret.), Yorkshire Regiment

A few weeks later, when my missile of a letter had not exploded, I had to assume that the editor of The Times had attended the same public school as Tom Maye. I decided to phone Pam.

'It's me, how's it going?'

'Well, I'm wrestling a bit with my poem, but how about your work?'

I decided to read to her an extract from my latest novel that I felt was rather good:

'The mountains rose through translucent blue mist and shimmered behind Giselle, plunging into the foaming sea, her sun-kissed body like a seal's pelt.'

'I thought it was a war novel.'

'I'm considering adding in a little romance.'

'But aren't you nearly finished, Geoffrey?'

'*Birdsong* was a best seller for Sebastian Faulks,' I said. 'Think of that, Pamela.'

I didn't want to talk about my 150,000-word novel, so I smokescreened and said I was missing my late wife's cooking. Later that evening, we met in The Fox for a drink. While Pam drilled down to the foundations of poetic form and her struggles with the sonnet, I spotted him.

'Shut up,' I said as I nudged her arm and nodded at him. 'Over there. Do you know who that is?'

'Well, he looks a bit familiar.'

'It's him, Pamela, the cliché terminator.'

I strode over.

When I tapped him on the shoulder, he looked up lazily.

'Can I help you?' he drawled, with those slack lips.

'May I ask you a question? Are you Tom Maye, the writer?' I said.

Irritation twitched across his face as he peeled away from the skinny redhead next to him.

'Yes, and who are you?'

'I'm Geoffrey Barnet, author.'

'Should I know you?'

'Well, you did read some of my work out on...' but, Pam shoved in with, 'Geoffrey, it's time to go. We're late.'

Later, after a scuffle, the police were called. 'I've found you out!' I shouted to him from the bouncer's headlock.

Unfortunately, I received a caution. And this is called a democratic society.

It was an arduous task, but I eventually located his address. He lived in a leafy area of Leeds. Approaching, I saw the house lights were out. Excellent. Concealed behind a tree, I pulled out my service binoculars. It began to rain. My balaclava readily absorbed the cold, fat drops that then ran down my neck, just like in the old days. It felt good, even though it was 23:00 hours before he screeched to a halt in his Vorsprung durch Technik. I waited until he was on his doorstep before I advanced.

'Good evening, Mr Maye. Could I talk to you for a moment?'

He turned with a, 'What the hell!' followed by, 'Not you again. What do you want now?'

'I recently heard you speaking on the radio, very clearly, on the subject of sloppy writing.'

'You did,' he said as he sidled towards the door and rested his hand on the white wall, the other on his hip, fingers drumming.

'Did you know you read from my manuscript as an example of bad writing?'

'Look here, old boy, I use all kinds of sources for...'

I butted in. 'Well, that may be, but I am an author, like you, except...'

I moved closer to him and said, '...I don't tell lies to inflate myself.'

He snorted.

'Inflate your ego, you mean, surely?' he said, laughing.

I continued. 'The cliché you are so vehemently against, well, I found one in your novel, *The Mote*.' I waved his novel and flicked open the page marked with a yellow sticky note.

'Here, where Johnny...'

He leaned over for a second and smirked. 'Johnny is a character who speaks in clichés. That's *his* language, not mine.'

He planted his hands on his hips and looked me in the eye.

'I don't care whose language it is. It's in here, and it's your novel.' I stabbed at the page.

'You didn't think that I would actually write *her writhing body*, did you?'

He laughed again. A thought moved behind his eyes before he planted his hand on my shoulder.

'I really think you should go home now, old chap.'

'Admit it, man, you wrote a damn cliché.'

'I'm going to call the police. Please get off my property.'

'You smug bastard!' I yelled, as an unfathomable rage blinded me. Advancing forward, I was back in my army days, pumping adrenalin, squaring the enemy, fighting defeat. I felled him backwards with a magnificent right hook. His scrawny head hit the wall, and he slithered down.

My case will be heard on January 9th 2023. I am accused of GBH. I have considered investigating the nature of irony in literature. However, my counsel has warned against this.

KIRKSTONE PASS

The mountains crowded around the petrified well on the ridge of Kirkstone Pass, their frosted tops pierced the clouds. Sarah bent to stare into the well.

'Careful! Don't fall in!' Jim grabbed her elbow.

'I can see something down there,' said Sarah.

Above, dark clouds glowered as sleet pelted down. Across from the pass, an old inn squatted. *Travellers Rest* read the inn's sign as it swung in the wind.

The couple scrambled to the door and heaved it open. Inside was hot and smoky. A fire raged in a nook. Hungry flames leapt and curled round fat, spitting logs. The low ceiling sagged from the weight of centuries past.

'What can I get you?' said a snowy-haired woman as she bustled towards them.

'A meal and a room for the night would be great.' Sarah yanked off her damp scarf and sat down.

'Well, you're in luck,' Helen, the landlady, laughed.

During their meal, Sarah and Jim quaffed a few pints of local ale and then collapsed into chairs and stared dreamily into the fire. Much later that evening, Helen bolted the doors and slid onto a chair next to Sarah and Jim to begin her story.

'Okay, kids.' She handed them both brimming glasses of whiskey. 'Here, in Kirkstone Pass, a long time ago, we had a tradition called "chase and catch". Every year, on the first Saturday in May, the young girls from the surrounding villages would gather at the top of the pass wearing their best bonnets. They did this to catch a husband.

Now, every Sunday, after church, my great-great-grandmother, Eleanor, used to step out in the company of Arthur Brackshaw. She was sixteen, he was seventeen, and what a pair they made. Eleanor always wore her cherry red silk bonnet because it set off her black curls.'

Helen paused to light a cigarette, breathed in and continued.

'Anyway, one day, in April 1886, the daffodils trembled in the light breeze as Arthur and Eleanor strolled around the village. A nervous Arthur remarked to Eleanor that, in his opinion, she would make a glorious catch for a lucky young man. And so, on the first Saturday in May, along with six other glowing girls from her village, Eleanor set off to take part in the chase and catch to be held at Kirkstone Pass. By then, she had set her mind on marrying Arthur. That Saturday, the weather was perfect for the chase. The sun radiated and the wind was high, already tugging at the colourful ribbons of the girls' bonnets as they scrambled in their sturdy boots. When they neared the top of the pass, Eleanor caught sight of Arthur standing by the inn with the other young men from the villages. They jostled and laughed, and Billy White even smoked a pipe in the manner of an older man. Eleanor glimpsed Arthur's waxed moustache and smiled. As she passed him, her cheeks pinked, so she lowered her gaze to her boots. Arthur tipped his hat after her and nudged the fellow next to him. Their chuckles echoed into the valley beyond.

The warmth of the spring sun could be felt between the gusting winds as the girls lined up along the ridge, their skirts billowing like sails. One by one, each girl turned to face the mountains while delicately undoing their bonnet ribbons, which fluttered in the bursts of wind. Each placed one hand on the top of their bonnet as they twirled around to face the row of grinning lads. And, when all the girls had turned, they freed their hats in one movement and began to run towards the inn, making a wish as they passed the well. Bonnets of all colours flew up into the air and were carried off by the spring blasts as the young men set chase. Red, yellow, green, blue, cerise, the bonnets bobbed along the heather. Some snagged on the thistles, while others were freed by the wind and carried on their journey. The girls ran in a steady line towards the inn. Their hopes grew with their quickened breaths. When they reached the inn, they lined up by the pocked walls and scrunched their handkerchiefs in anxiety.'

Behind Helen, the fire blazed in the dark grate. She turned briefly to warm her hands before continuing.

'A rule of the contest was that the bonnet must be in perfect order for it to be returned to its owner. Those clumsy young men who damaged the hats as they snatched them from the thistles were disqualified. The triumphant ones returned with their catch and stood around preening. Once all were assembled, they whisked out their bonnet for its blushing owner to step forward to reclaim. This gesture acted as a proposal of marriage. Arthur flashed the green bonnet he had chased and grinned at Eleanor so his face might crack. Eleanor stood rooted. Stretching his smile so it hurt and nodding towards her, he extended the bonnet further out. But, still, Eleanor was motionless as she stared at Lucy, who stumbled slowly towards Arthur, her face set in a rigid smile as she placed her hands on her green hat. Arthur jerked his head round to catch Eleanor's eye, but saw she was now heading towards Jonas Ashworth, with a smile as stiff as frozen grass. Jonas held out Eleanor's cherry red bonnet.

'Oh, no!' Sarah blurted. Behind Helen, the fire's flames had shrunk and transformed into brittle embers. She continued.

'On that day, Eleanor discovered Arthur was colour blind.'

'How awful, don't you think so, Jim?' Sarah nudged her husband, whose eyes had closed. His legs sprawled out under the bench.

'There's more.' Helen lifted the whiskey bottle to assess its contents.

'Kirkstone Pass had been chosen because it was very windy at that time of year. Consequently, not all bonnets were caught, resulting in some girls remaining unmarried until the next year, and, for some, the next and the next as they gradually became old maids. This suited their farmer fathers, of course, who wanted them to stay at home to help chase the sheep from the tops. This was the fate of Spinster Mary, who, each year, after the event, would scour the mountain foot for the bonnets that had evaded the suitors, and were now snared only by brambles. People said she sold them at the market to support her fragile income.

Now, my great-great-grandmother Eleanor was a practical girl and made of her life what she could. Jonas was hard working and hard drinking. "The agile elbow", she sometimes called him. But, one freezing night, stumbling home, he rested under a tree and failed to wake up the following morning. However, he had saved money to make a modest investment, and Eleanor came into a small inheritance two weeks after she had thrown soil on the top of his cloth coffin. At this time, the inn by the ridge was up for sale. Eleanor bought it and ran it for weathered travellers on their harsh journeys to Penrith markets.

The following spring, Eleanor was on her way to the next village to buy curtain material. She passed a tumbledown cottage with a caved-in roof. Eleanor knew it had been the home of Spinster Mary. She stepped in to see if there was anything salvageable. In a corner, a rusted tin chest crouched. Eleanor released its cracked lid. Inside, a jumble of old bonnets lay. She caught her breath and scooped them up into a threadbare blanket she found slung over a decayed mattress. Later that night, as the moon floated over the mountain peaks, Eleanor took her bundle, unfurled it, and, one by one, hurled the hats into the inn's wishing well, her whole body shuddering with the force of her sobs. All night, she slumped over the edge of the well and dripped corrosive tears onto the unclaimed bonnets. Some of them had fallen awkwardly and, in their frustrated descent, clung to the well's sides. Over the years, they became petrified. Locals said that Eleanor's tears were the cause of this.'

Helen raised her glass and emptied it.

'So that's the story, and now, my lovelies, it's time for bed.' She nodded towards Jim, who needed Sarah to nudge him awake.

'Oh, sorry,' he said, opening his eyes and rubbing them.

The couple wobbled to their feet. Behind them, the orange embers had crumbled into fragile layers that, by dawn, would be cold, grey ashes.

The next morning, Sarah stepped out into the bracing air to take one last look at the well that had now become an emblem of torn, abandoned dreams. She stared hard into its darkness for some time. When she looked up, the glaring sun dazzled her, plunging her into momentary blindness. As her vision returned, she scanned the ridge. Along the mountain's foot, she thought she glimpsed hundreds of snagged fragments of cloth, like coloured ribbons waving in the fresh breeze.

COCKTAILS WITH MARIE, 1994

A September gale blew in with me as I pushed open the glass and steel doors of the cocktail bar. Zigzag neon lights winked on and off across the dark red walls. The place was humid and smoky as I struggled over to where Marie was sitting. She was blowing plumes of blue smoke into the air, a pair of Ray-Bans perched on her head, like an Alice band. I swear she slept in them. Here was my stepsister planning her wedding to Henry. It was to be a grand affair, a statement about how well they had done and how this would continue. A pointed, prickling performance to be envied.

'So what do you think?' she asked.

Bride Magazine was open on the table for me to admire. I took my seat. Marie had placed her index finger on a spectacular dress, a cream silk frothy thing of epic proportions. I wanted to say Princess Diana has a lot to answer for, but a quick look at Marie's expression killed my thought.

'Well, it's a bit...' I stopped to rethink my response and shrugged out of my grey linen coat.

'What?' Marie's lips pursed tight. I had to admit that she really did have cute bow lips.

'Sort of, traditional,' I mumbled.

'I'm not a lefty like you.' Marie pulled back from the table edge, and guilt stabbed me in the stomach.

'No, it's a lovely dress. It's very you.'

I could feel myself start to perspire, and I began to worry that I would forever say the wrong thing in her presence. After all, she had been Mum's favourite; blood is thicker than water.

Marie snapped her fingers at a nearby waiter, whose floppy fringe kept falling across his eyes as he bent down to take orders. He nodded and quickly glided to our table, whisked out his pen and pad and asked, 'What would you ladies like?'

'Two margaritas, please,' Marie said.

'Anything else?'

'Yes!' She looked at his wrist, seemingly distracted. 'That's a nice watch.'

He puffed up slightly and smiled.

'Is it a *real* Rolex,' she continued, leaning over to peer at his watch and then at him.

The waiter mimicked a laugh, but did not reply to her. As he whizzed away with our order, she turned to me and said, 'Turkish market trash, probably.'

'Honestly!' I looked at her. 'Don't be so snotty!'

'Don't you be such a sucker! If he can't afford a real Rolex, he should downsize his image.'

Marie waved one hand in the air to dismiss my feelings and started to flick the pages of the magazine with the other. 'Look,' she said, giving me an enormous, face-cracking grin that made the tiniest wrinkles appear under her eyes, just for a second. After all, she was twenty-six now, a mature bride. I chuckled to myself.

'Bridesmaids dresses!' She squealed and wiggled her petite nose. She had a nose plastic surgeons would imitate, but hers was real. Marie was engrossed in admiration for a puce, bubbly number. It looked to me like something Cinderella might appear in at the top of the stairs, in a Disney blow-out film. Or a frock a drag act might wear, exaggerated glamour that quietly mocked femininity.

'I..' I shrugged and pulled a smile of sorts. What could I say?

'I'm thinking,' she said as the waiter twirled into view and began putting out mats for our drinks. 'Six bridesmaids in lines of two.'

She drew imaginary lines on the marble table-top with two pointed manicured nails. 'And I'd like you to be one.'

'Lovely margaritas,' I coughed into my drink. *Why me?* I thought. Stepsister or not, how could I put one of those things on? And what would I look like?

'So?' She looked me in the eye. I could feel my shoulders rising in protection; an animal reflex.

'That's so sweet of you, Marie, it really is, but...'

'But, what?' She banged down her drink, sloshing it over her side of the table.

I reached out my hand to hers but she pulled away.

'Marie, I just can't imagine myself in...' I pointed to the puce confection, '...well, one of those.'

There was silence for a moment. Something flashed behind her eyes. She put out her hand to pat mine.

'It's not a problem, Ava.' She continued to pat, nodding her head so that her sleek bob shook slightly, but the sunglasses stayed put.

'Thanks, that's great.' I relaxed a little. Relieved.

'No, really.' She looked steadily at me with her hard black eyes. 'You being fat isn't a problem.'

I choked on my drink. 'Pardon?'

'We can work on it. Go to the gym every day.' She was snapping her fingers for the waiter again.

After a few seconds of silence, I asked, 'What about my bad back?'

'Not that again, Ava. You've used it all your life. Give it a rest,' she said. 'Besides, exercise never hurt anyone.' An air hostess smile stretched across her mouth.

'Really?' I snorted. 'Jane Fonda had a heart attack feeling the burn.'

'I'll lend you my workout videos.' She appeared unruffled and reached for her drink. The frosted glass glinted in the winking lights.

'I don't do exercise.'

Marie made a show of looking me up and down.' You're fat because you're lazy.'

'That's your opinion.'

'How much do you weigh step-sis?' She leaned closer.

'Thirteen stone.' I couldn't believe I'd told her. 'Happy now?'

'That's a bit much for someone not very tall.'

I wanted to punch her right there, in the yuppie cocktail bar full of rich, smug people like her. Instead, I glugged my drink and scraped my chair back.

'You can keep your body fascism!'

I stood up and yanked my coat from the back of the plastic chair. The waiter was back with more drinks perched on a tray.

'Have one on me,' I said to him, before I rushed to the Ladies' room in tears.

After I had wiped my mascara-smeared cheeks, blown my nose and adjusted my skirt, I decided to call a taxi. I approached the public phone and saw Marie inside, speaking to someone. I neared and heard her say, 'It worked, Henry. She won't be coming.'

THE BABA YAGA TREE

Poland

At the edge of the village, on the skirts of the forest, a twisted tree struggled up in a tangle from the dry, red earth. The wind rushed through its gnarled branches. It looked like a tree of hissing snakes, some villagers said. Others said that it had been cursed by the Baba Yaga long ago when love abandoned her, and she took to sorcery. She still lived somewhere in the heart of the forest, they said. Her crooked fingers could cast spells that would maim even the most beautiful. The villagers whispered that one gaze from her black, beady eyes could curdle the freshest goat's milk.

The tree's gnarled bough was probably shaped by the relentless wind, rain and snow that whipped across the land in the winter months slapped by the ferocious, ancient elements that moved across the earth. Or, perhaps, passing Cossacks had once stopped and ripped off the fledgling branches to feed their fires before bedding down on the frozen ground. They would have huddled around the crackling heat, dreaming of beautiful Polish girls with golden hair while their horses snorted into the icy night air and red sparks flew up into the sky.

Pozam Village, August 1939

Roman and Andrej played football on the village outskirts with a rotting cabbage Old Petrevski had thrown to his pigs. Two ten-year-olds, their trousers held up with string. Andrej rushed towards the cabbage and kicked hard with his tanned, bare foot. The cabbage shot into the air and landed beneath the Baba Yaga tree.

'Yes!' Andrej shouted, throwing his arms up and dancing triumphantly around in circles, raising small dust clouds. Roman cuffed Andrej's head as he jogged past him to retrieve the ball. 'Tchah! That's bad luck!' he said.

'What is?'

'The Baba Yaga tree. It's cursed, and we've got to keep away from it,' Roman said, as he dangled his slender arm over Andrej's bony shoulder.

'Phooey! Old wives tales. For cissy girls and children.'

'No, it's not!' Roman said. 'She still lives in the forest. My grandmother says so.'

A mischievous expression crossed Andrej's face. 'Okay, Roman, I dare you to come with me to find her tonight, if she exists?'

Later, the boys crept from their homes into the rustling night. As they pushed through spiked undergrowth, startled animals sprinted away. In the distance, a deer cried and then fled. Its hooves scrambled the ground. Deeper into the forest they ventured and eventually came across a low light that fell through the trees. As they came nearer, a tumbledown shack emerged in dark outline. The lads scrambled up a tree for a better view. Balanced on the highest branches of an oak tree, they strained to see what was inside the shack. A grey form huddled over a lamp and worked at something with its head bent low. It was an old woman.

'It's her. It's her, the Baba Yaga!' Roman said, and grabbed at his friend in a rush of excitement. But the sudden movement threw Andrej off balance. He swayed on his branch then dropped from the tree into a bed of nettles, letting out a piercing yelp.

Roman froze as he saw the figure in the shack rise and move towards the door. 'Run, Andrej!' he shouted to his friend below. Roman scrambled down the tree trunk and sliced his knee on the rough bark.

Andrej hopped out from the nettle bed just as the old woman's outline appeared at the door. A dim light wavered behind her. 'Who's there?' she demanded, pulling her shawl tighter around her neck.

Crouching on the ground, Andrej fumbled around, resting his hand on what felt like a heavy stone.

'You old witch!' he cried as he stood and hurled the stone that struck her hard on her soft, left temple. Blood trickled down her wrinkled cheek as the tiny widow crumpled to the floor with a moan.

September 1939

Roman idly flicked crumbs from the table as the family ate their breakfast of rye bread and dried sausage. Outside their home, the birds cried and circled above the still trees. He heard their final squawks before they flapped off into the clouded sky. Then an unfamiliar rumbling began. Roman raised his head to look out of the window as army vehicles roared into the village.

'What is it?' his mother said as she lowered her chipped cup from her lips.

Trucks loaded with German soldiers sped past their window, rifles balanced on their knees. The chickens scattered and the geese honked and flapped, but the soldiers laughed and jostled one another as they bounced along the stony road. Two motorbikes followed them, raising dust along the path into the small village. As Roman's family watched from their window, the trucks circled and halted at the well. An officer, whose mouth resembled a thin gash, swung open his truck door and signalled to the young soldiers, who scattered across the village like scolded rats. They hastily emptied the village houses and herded their bewildered occupants to the well. The officer introduced himself to the assembled villagers as Colonel Steinberg. He jutted out his weak chin as he shouted.

'From today, this village is declared part of Germany!' He lifted his cap and patted his thinned hair. 'German families are on their way to reclaim our land. It was our land before, and now it will be again.'

The villagers stood motionless.

'Heil Hitler!' Officer Steinberg shouted and saluted, quickly followed by his men. 'Your houses will become ours, for our families. You,' he stabbed his finger at the crowd, 'will come with us. Schnell!'

'What?' cried a woman whose broad shoulders strained her ragged shawl.

'Be silent, cabbage face!' Steinberg shouted.

'Please! We want to stay in our homes,' she said.

'Frau, I have told you....' But something cut the officer short. A flop-eared dog sprang from the crowd, pushing his snout between Steinberg's knees. The dog sniffed inquisitively at the officer's crotch. Steinberg glanced down then kicked him away. The dog yelped, cowered back for an instant, then rushed forward and clamped his jaws on the officer's knee, growling. Roman's father was unable to stifle his amusement as his shoulders shook.

'You! What's so funny?' Steinberg screamed as he tried to shrug the dog off with an awkward, kicking motion. His face tightened into a rictus and reddened.

'Nothing!' Roman's father spluttered, slightly out of control.

Steinberg raised his arm, pointed his pistol at the dog and shot him point blank. The dog slumped to the floor. The villagers were silent, but Roman's father stretched out both hands in a questioning gesture.

'What?' said Steinberg as he aimed his pistol at him. 'Do you have something to say?'

'No, sir!' Roman's father said, his face rigid.

'Good!' said Steinberg as he pulled the trigger of his gun.

'No!' Roman cried out as his father, with a look of utter surprise, his hat cocked, crumpled to the ground. Blood spurted onto the hard earth from a neat bullet hole in the centre of his forehead. The soldiers began herding the villagers, knocking down the older and slower ones. 'Polish peasant!' one said as he kicked Roman's mother to the ground. Then, the shooting began.

Rozdeyck Labour Camp, Poland, 1943

A feeble spring sun fell on Roman as he toiled the barren soil. The weak heat somehow stirred a glimmer of hope within him that had been buried beneath layers of miserable hard labour over the last four years. He had almost forgotten how to feel anything.

Roman stretched his skeletal frame to raise his bowed head towards the sun. His gaze moved from the cracked, broken ground beneath him, up and over the barbed fence, to the forest beyond. He recalled that the forest had been where dark things flitted or pounced in his childhood - a place of fear. But, now, the forest was a place of light and hope, to where some prisoners had escaped and disappeared into the deep dark green.

Roman's gaze fell on a lone, gnarled tree. Its crooked branches twisted up towards a blank, uncaring sky. Roman remembered the Baba Yaga tree of his youth. He recalled the night he and Andrej snuck into the forest to find the witch of the old fairy tales, and how he had invaded the old woman's shack. Inside the hovel, the fire's dying embers had smouldered in a blackened grate. A pot that hung over it still spat and sizzled as steam coiled into the musty air. Shrivelled herbs dangled from the ceiling and emitted a fetid smell. In one corner, a lumpy mattress squatted, covered with a ragged quilt made from scraps of cloth. He recalled an ancient cat that had raised its wobbling head to peer through clouded eyes. It had opened its toothless mouth and released a croaky mew. *A witch's cat*, he had thought. He remembered staring around the room at the bundles of rags heaped on the floor. He had sought evidence of witchcraft in the Baba Yaga's lair, but there was none. Roman marched across to kick the rags around, and ran to the door, gripped by fear and fury.

His face was now fiery with shame as he remembered grabbing a sputtering candle and hurling it into the bundled rags. 'Baba Yaga, witch!' he spat out as he jumped over the old woman's body, slumped at her door and fled into the night while her shack flared up, throwing red embers into the night sky.

Now, Roman turned to the other camp where the grey ones toiled - the ones he had barely noticed, so deep was he in his own suffering. They were shaven, starved shadows of human beings. He looked at their camp's elevated chimney, belching thick, foul smoke into the sky. Under the piercing clarity of the midday sun, Roman saw the fine grey powder that covered everything and the pungent, acrid air made his eyes smart with tears.

Baba Yaga is a mythological witch from Polish and Russian folklore. As children, our Polish father told us stories about her at bedtime! The village and camp are fictional, but events from the Second World War inspired my story.

An edited version of this story first appeared in The Looking Glass Anthology, Volume Six, published by the Looking Glass Society of the University of York in 2016.

FACE OFF

She said, 'Face your demons. Free yourself.'

'Rather eat a live snake than talk about it,' I'd quip. But her bags were packed, so, pushing fifty, I rocked up at the Christmas Phobia Workshop in a mansion on the moors. It was snowing. The bare winter trees were disappearing fast under a soft white blanket. Outside, the sky flooded amethyst and silver with the sinking winter light. Inside, a log fire crackled and spat. Anabel nestled in a creaking Chesterfield, welcoming each of us as we took our seats. I was a little late.

She began. 'I want to reassure you that what goes on here remains here.'

A fat guy called Clint interrupted her, 'How can you be so sure of that?' He leaned into the circle, one hand angled on his knee, elbow jutting.

'We have to trust one another.' Anabel scrutinised the assembled group and tossed her tie dye silk scarf over one shoulder. 'Because you have all agreed to tell your stories.'

Clint waggled his foot and flicked something imaginary off his knee.

'Clint, would you like to start?'

He grimaced. 'I'm only here because my wife says she'll divorce me if I don't sort it.'

'That's weak,' said Anabel.

So, Clint told us that the reason he hated Christmas was because it was a big fat con. He said it was 'cruel on poor people and, after all, it's just one day'.

Anabel interrupted him. 'Many people would agree, but isn't there something more?'

'This is hard.' Clint pulled at the neck of his jumper.

'Maybe there's an incident?' Anabel prompted.

'Okay, yeah, I mean it was Christmas Eve. I was just a kid.' Clint passed a shaky hand over his face. 'Mum and Dad were out shopping. I decided to decorate the tree with candles.' He faltered.

'That's a German tradition,' I said, hoping to help him through.

'We weren't Krauts,' he snapped. 'That's not the story. We lived in the country. We had tons of power cuts and stacks of candles. Anyway, the tree caught fire while I was out chopping wood, then the curtains flared, then the sofa burst into flames, then the house ignited. Granny was upstairs asleep. She perished. Burnt to a crisp.'

I had an urge to laugh, but coughed instead.

'That's terrible.' Anabel shook her head at Clint, who sat back and folded his arms over his chest and said, 'That's me done.'

'Hmm, perhaps.'

Anabel asked if anyone else cared to share. A ginger-haired woman shot up her hand. Her name was Marilyn. She said when she was eleven her mother died on Christmas morning. Pneumonia. Marilyn had three brothers and one baby sister. As the eldest, she was forced to cook Christmas dinner. She'd only ever cooked rhubarb crumble in domestic science class. Marilyn burned the turkey causing the cooker to catch light.

'The cooker?' I shouted.

Anabel raised her hand to shut me up. Marilyn continued. In a fit, her grieving father threw her and the cindered dinner out in to the snow. She could still see it melting around the blackened mass and turning a greasy brown shade. She's never eaten Christmas dinner since, she told us.

'That's nothing!' a black-haired woman with aggressive eyebrows shouted. Her name was Joan. 'Listen to this!' She was fired up. Joan said, 'At seventeen, I married and cooked my first Christmas dinner. I forgot to defrost the turkey on Christmas Eve. So, early Christmas morning, while the others snored off their hangovers, I ran it under the hot tap for an hour. My hands were red raw. When the turkey was soft and pink, I shoved it in the oven. My morning sickness lingered so I didn't eat much. After dinner, my husband and his gruesome family became ill, projectile vomit everywhere. Later, they all died in hospital. Listeria it was. I was bequeathed the family fortune. But a spiteful relative asked the police to investigate. They concluded I poisoned them to inherit so I went to prison for seven years.'

Ginger Marilyn said that was pretty bad but *she* hadn't finished yet. After the turkey incident, she told us, her father had a nervous breakdown and couldn't look after his family.

Marilyn ran away from home and was later taken into care. A couple adopted her. Trouble was they were obsessed with Christmas and celebrated all year round. She became vegetarian to avoid the stinking turkey dinners. When Marilyn was fifteen, she couldn't stand it anymore so she murdered the adoptive fanatics then ran away to Canada.

'How did you murder them?' I asked before I could stop myself. Marilyn said it was easy. She stole tranquilisers from the chemist's where she worked Saturdays and crushed them into mulled wine. Once they'd died, she slow-roasted her adoptive parents over a spit in the yard. They lived in the wilds so she fed them to the wolves, telling the authorities they disappeared one freezing night.

Stunned, I looked over at Anabel who sat nodding her head, a slight smile on her lips.

A blond man with restless legs raised his arm. He suggested we move away from Christmas roasts. Anabel said it was up to him. His name was Brad. He told us that one Christmas he decided to mail himself to his granny because he hated his parents' seasonal decorations. The label fell off the package and he ended up in Greenland.

'That's not possible!' I blurted.

'Don't interrupt others!' Anabel warned.

Brad said he was taken into child slavery, a sweatshop, forced to make Christmas toys for eighteen hours a day for seven years, before he escaped. 'That's how I lost my finger,' he said, holding up a four-digit hand.

'This is bullshit!' I yelled, standing up and throwing my hands in the air. 'I can't tell my story, it's too, well...too bland.'

'It's part of storytelling to feel apprehensive,' Anabel said.

'What do you mean storytelling?'

'Where do you think you are?' Anabel asked.

'The Christmas Phobia Workshop,' I said.

The group burst out laughing. Anabel stood up to catch my elbow as I rushed from the room. 'You're in the Liar's Workshop, Christmas Special.' I froze.

Then I realised I could tell my story. Get it off my chest at last. 'One Christmas Eve,' I began, 'I crept downstairs to peek at the presents but instead I found my mother kissing Santa.'

'That's a Christmas song,' sniped Clint.

'Shut it!' I barked. I told them the trouble was Santa was actually Sandra, my Mum's best friend. I was confused and upset so I squealed to Dad. He was cool about it and said, 'Keep this between us, Jodie.' He tapped his nose. Christmas Day went smoothly. On Boxing Day, he threw Mum out, bags flying into the snow. I never saw her again. The group clapped. Anabel said not bad for a beginner.

As I walked down the corridor, I passed a sign on a red door saying *Christmas Phobia Workshop Cancelled Because of Bad Weather*. Outside, I skidded over the frozen ground towards my red Mini. I felt as though I might float away. Above me the stars winked in the inky sky as I pulled out my phone and called my girlfriend. 'How did it go babe?' she asked.

'You wouldn't believe it,' I said.

WILD NIGHT

'Can you help me fix this?'

Boy, was it my lucky day? A beautiful blonde leaned into a smoking engine beneath its gaping hood.

'I can try.' "Modesty" is my middle name. I strode towards her and she stepped elegantly out of the way, passing a slim hand over her dampened forehead. Moving in close, I could see that the engine had overheated. Simple. I had to think fast but she pre-empted me. 'I live nearby. If we could just get her back to my place that would be great.' She smiled full-on at me. This blonde had to be a model. I swear my knees felt unsubstantial for my body.

'You look in shape.' She threw her glance up and down my body. 'Perhaps we could push together?'

It wasn't impossible. 'How far do you live?' I managed to stutter.

'Just round that corner, up ahead,' she replied, nodding to the road. I began calculating how I could slip out my mobile to cancel tonight's game with the guys, without appearing presumptuous. Jesus, those legs of hers went on forever. We walked round to the back of the grounded Citroën and began to push. 'She used to belong to my grandma.' She stunned me with that smile again. It was a grey day but the sun came out.

'Oh yeah!' I chirped. Being an orphan, I hadn't known a grandma but understood people were very attached to that generation of their clan.

'Gran left it to me when she died. I hardly ever use it, but fancied a drive out today.'

I nearly said, 'Well, you didn't get very far,' but I thought that sounded sneery. 'Is that why it's a *she*?'

'Yes, her name's Daisy, like my gran.'

I was just about to ask her name when a guy passing stopped. 'Need help?' His eyes travelled up and down my stunning damsel-in-distress. 'I know you.'

Anger flared in my chest.

'No, we're fine,' she said, with those cherry lips. She winked at me. The guy lingered for a short while, scratching at his head. Oh, boy, I really should be cancelling tonight's game. My phone bulged in my pocket.

Somehow, we managed to push her car around the corner.

'I live here.' Angel-face pointed to a block of flats. 'You've been so kind. Would you like to come in for a cup of coffee or something?'

I asked myself if I'd really woken up that day. I pinched my arm and, yes, it was real.

'That'd be great.' I followed her through the front entrance trying not to gambol like an excited puppy. In the lift, we stood quite close and I could feel the heat from her body. Tiny drops of perspiration twinkled on her upper lip. She looked like Debbie Harry, but even more beautiful, if you can, for a second, imagine that. The lift jolted on the sixth floor. 'Here we are.' She gestured for me to go first and I staggered out.

The décor inside her flat was a little clinical for my tastes, but I managed to mumble, 'Minimalist right?' as I sat on the steel and leather sofa, as directed. There were no cushions, fluffy rugs, or soft toys.

'Tea or coffee?' Blondie stood in front of me with her hands spread over curved hips.

'First, I'd like to know your name?' I felt a blush burn my cheeks.

'Ivy. Hate it myself but it's stuck.' She let out a muffled cackle.

Her fresh delivery contrasted with the toying games of so many women I'd met.

'My name's Jerry.'

Ivy leaned over and her cleavage peeped from the rim of her blouse. Lush, plump.

'I have some excellent brandy too, if you like?'

While Ivy made coffee, I got up and strolled around her living room. All the surfaces gleamed. The pale grey walls were hung with just a few framed prints: Dali's *Christ's Crucifixion,* Munch's *The Scream* (which I had only ever seen as a cartoon on t-shirts), and Caravaggio's *The Beheading of John the Baptist.* I wondered if granny Daisy had bequeathed these ghastly depictions, too. Ivy swivelled back into the room and plonked down right next to me, smiling, handing me my coffee with a little extra.

Later, when I opened my eyes, it was dark and I didn't know where I was until I heard that cackle followed by, 'Let's have some fun!'

I stared in disbelief. My hands and feet were shackled to the steel bedstead by razor wire. If I moved at all, it seared into my flesh. Trickles of blood already ran down my wrists, forming rivulets on the white sheet.

'What the fuck's going on?' I shouted. 'I haven't done anything.'

Ivy lit a candle and moved towards me. She held the candle under her chin to create a distorted image of her face.

'Don't you want to know what I want?' There was a lightness in her voice that made me think maybe this was a really weird joke.

'Yes, tell me, please.' I sounded pathetic.

She moved to the bedside and pushed her hand under the mattress. She tugged and I heard the clink of metal. 'You have a choice between losing your dick or your balls. Which is it to be?'

I almost laughed. It was so absurd. But she saw and stabbed the knife into the pillow. 'Don't laugh at me, Mr Superior. You're the dummy. Didn't your mother tell you never to talk to strangers?'

'Well, as a child...'

'Don't judge a book by its cover,' she sneered. 'There's no such thing as a free lunch.'

'Did something bad happen to you, Ivy?' I struggled to remember my training. Get her talking.

'Not anything really bad.' She ran her finger down the blade of the knife. 'Just annoying.'

'Annoying? Like how?' My whole body was trembling. 'Nobody takes me seriously.'

'What?'

'You know what I mean. They see a set of features.' She stared hard at me and held the knife blade to her cheek. 'I can hurt you or I can hurt myself. Your choice.'

'I'm not playing, you mad bitch.'

'Fine!' She stepped back. 'I'll see you tomorrow.'

That night was long. My phone rang intermittently, the guys wondering where I was. It was impossible to move without serious injury. The gag around my mouth muffled any noise I tried to make. Eventually, I drifted into fitful sleep.

Later, the increased traffic noise told me it was daytime. My stomach rumbled, but my mouth was parched and my tongue resembled a dried slug. The door swung open. Ivy entered, wearing red satin Capri pants and kitten heels. She completed the movie-star look with heart-shaped sunglasses. She moved towards me, and her heels clicked on the tiles. *Easy to clean*, she'd remarked last night. Ivy brandished wire cutters. Leaning over and cutting my feet free she said, 'You're no fun. But if you report me to the police, I'll find you and finish you off.' She paused and looked me over. 'Shame, because you're quite hot.' The wire cutters crunched and my arms were free. I dropped them to my side and lay motionless, like an animal playing dead. Ivy leaned over and kissed my forehead. She turned and disappeared.

I staggered home. My phone rang as I slammed the front door shut.

'Jerry, where were you last night?' Frank asked.

'You won't believe me,' I guffawed and flumped down on my sofa. 'Tied to a bed by a beautiful blonde.'

'In your dreams mate.'

'Really... what a wildcat she was.' I clicked the TV on as we talked. Ivy's picture flashed above a news banner: 'Dangerous escapee... do not approach.'

AREA 523

'They pay well,' Axel says as he slaps a piece of paper with a number on it into my palm. He folds into the rain-drenched night and I scuttle back home. In my apartment, the natural light has drained from the sky outside. I squint to stab the number into the phone. My services are cut off as I'm broke. From the gloom, I hear a woman ask me, 'How may I help you?'

My words tumble out. 'Put me through to HR.' Kraftwerk thrums on the line as I wait to be transferred.

'Which procedure are you interested in, madam?' a soporific voice asks as I spot a ship drop below the skyline and then land. More on their way, I assume.

'I'm thinking the special research programme.'

'Freshers, we call it.' There's a sneer in her voice. 'As a ground-breaking intervention it attracts the highest price.'

I've played the scenario over and over in my mind, kicking back tangled sheets on hot nights. It's my only way out. But still a spark of curiosity ignites in me.

'Where do they come from?'

Shit, it just slips out. There's a pause on the line, a stifled sigh. 'We don't disclose such information but assure rearing in the strictest of conditions.'

'They're not free range then.' My joke is outrageous.

'It's safe, humane. I can put you in contact with our counselling function if you like – many volunteers seek reassurance at this point.'

'No.'

·········

I trudge down a white, cell-lined corridor, behind which muffled cries seep out. On each door there is a blinking security pad. I want to stop and open one to peer inside, but the assistant turns to beckon me forward. As I near the end of the corridor, light slides from underneath a double door. The motion sensors swing it open into a stainless-steel room that is lit so harshly I must shade my eyes. Very soon, my sight clears to focus on a lumpy mass that lies on a table, beneath a silver blanket. It twitches. Cloudy yellow and red tubes trail from underneath the cover to an adjoining bed, ready to be attached. I know I am to steal, but from what? I shake and sweat but cannot stop now. I propel myself forward to the waiting bed. I've heard they're grown in dank half-light, off-planet, in space, and arrive here ready to be snapped off and absorbed, rebirthed. It's a privilege to merge with those like me. To live, as life should, overground. To breathe in the clean air beneath the sun and sky. Before my heavy eyelids close, I see a red sign flashes above the door: Human Resources Area 523 A voice says, 'Get down now Rex, good boy.' I hear soft pads on the floor followed by another voice. 'Okay, let's start with the heart. Poor sucker, it's you who's paying the highest price.'

HEY JOE

'Should've seen Joe Platt down Greengates Village yesterday. Practically swinging a handbag he was.' My mother nodded her head affirmatively, a twinkle in her eye. Her friend, Molly, laughed and took a deep drag on a cigarette, before she stubbed it out in the overflowing glass ashtray, perched on the edge of the wooden draining board.

'It's his dad's fault you know, Jenny,' said Molly. 'Even their Alsatian's scared of him.'

'Ah, now, that's true,' said Mum reaching for another Capstan Full Strength from the pack on the Formica worktop. She and Molly were standing in our kitchen gossiping about the neighbours. It was a boiling day at the beginning of August, 1966. During that hallowed summer, everyone was happy because on the thirtieth of July, England won the World Cup. The weather was sweltering; too hot even to play outside in the garden for very long. I slipped into the kitchen to grab a cream soda ice lolly from the tray in our new fridge. My friends were amazed we could make our own lollies. I plonked myself on the stool in a corner, underneath the shelf where the wireless rested. It was on at a low hum with a faint light beneath the cloudy screen. The green vinyl stool cover stuck to the top of my legs and squeaked slightly as I wriggled around trying to cool down. I was seven years old.

'Can lads have handbags?' I asked. The two women swopped amused glances.

'Never you mind! You should be out in the fresh air, madam,' my mother said, with a smile, as she crossed the red linoleum floor to rouse me from the stool. As I skipped out of the kitchen, Molly said, 'Jenny, did you know that Mick Jagger's from Middlesex.' And they both fell about laughing.

Our garden backed onto three other neighbours' gardens, one on each side and one at the bottom, separated by flimsy wire fences, threaded through ugly concrete posts the corporation supplied when the houses were rapidly built during the 1950s. That was five years after the war, during the baby boom of expansion and optimism, beneath which an obscure fear still lurked. I could see Joe Platt lounging in a deck chair through our back fence, sunbathing with his shirt open to the waist. He wore tight, dog-tooth, hipster trousers looped by a thick white belt. His long legs were crossed at the ankles, his feet encased in suede Cuban-heeled boots. A red and white transistor radio nestled in his lap, playing Radio Caroline, a pirate radio station that broadcast non-stop pop music, which my dad sometimes listened to. A cigarette dangled from one of Joe's hands that draped lazily over the top of his head. His eyes were obscured by sunglasses, and I worried he was asleep in the heat and that his cigarette might drop from his fingers and singe his blond curls. I dawdled on our swing, watching him for a while. It pleased me to look at his almost girlish face. But then his father burst into their garden with fists clenched at his sides. Their Alsatian ran behind him, barking and circling.

'What the fuck are you doing, you long-haired lout?' He whacked Joe over the ear. 'Get the hell inside and button your shirt up. You're a disgrace.'

Joe jumped up and flicked his cigarette into the unkempt grass teeming with nettles.

'And get that bleeding hair of yours cut. Yer look like a lass,' Mr Platt bawled at Joe's scrambling figure retreating inside. He stomped off towards his outhouse, with the dog following behind, slinking low to the ground.

On January 4th, 1969, I perched on our sofa watching Lulu on TV with my parents. I adored the Lulu show. She wore height-of-fashion clothes, completely unavailable in provincial cities; Swinging London clothes I ached to wear at age eleven. Outfits I tried to replicate for my Tressy doll with limited success, using cloth remnants from my mother's sewing box. Lulu sang and danced in white calf-hugging boots. Happening new guests were premiered on her show. She was plugged-in. That Saturday, she introduced us to the Jimi Hendrix Experience. Jimi wore crushed velvet flares strained across his hips, and a balloon sleeved shirt under an embroidered waistcoat. The band started to play 'Hey Joe', their psychedelic chart hit. My father lurched forward in his seat about to say something and the plastic sofa creaked. Jimi kept glancing at his bandmates. He nodded and they abruptly stopped playing. The camera was zooming in and out as Jimi announced, 'We're gonna stop playing this rubbish.' They launched into a tribute to the newly disbanded supergroup, Cream, of which I was dimly aware. The camera was going wild, swinging around, unsure of who to focus on, as 'Sunshine of Your Love' exploded from their guitars, a cacophony of sounds I had never heard before that thrilled me even more than *The Outer Limits*. My father leapt up from the sofa. The air in our front room was electric. He bunched his fists by his side, shouting, 'Turn them off!' But he was rooted to the spot, transfixed by the TV, appalled at the fearless generation who were taking control in front of his eyes on a BBC light entertainment show. For him, a frightening new order was emerging.

When the song had finished, the camera panned to the stunned live audience, who had to be reminded to clap by someone behind the scenes. Lulu managed to smile while saying something polite. My father stamped out of the room. He left the house and rode on his Honda scooter into the freezing night. It was just past nine, but Mum sent my sister and me to bed, saying, 'Well, that's enough shenanigans for the night.' She was Irish and later I would recall her sayings with a smile.

In August, 1969, the British Army was deployed on the streets of Northern Ireland as the Troubles erupted. Joe Platt joined the army that summer. 'I hope it sorts him out,' my father said to my mother when he heard the news.

'I hope the Brits sort them out,' she said, getting up from the breakfast table before we'd finished and leaving the room. She was Irish, after all.

At nineteen, I moved to Leeds to university. It was the end of the punk era, when boyfriends and girlfriends shared kohl eyeliner and black nail polish to outrage the establishment. When my first year ended, I moved from safe student accommodation into a run-down Victorian house with my boyfriend, Julian, and three other students. Julian, or Jools, as he preferred, was astoundingly good-looking, and I couldn't quite believe he'd chosen me. He had an acute mind, but was pathologically shy. For the two years we lived in the house, he spent most of his time in our room, reading Jean-Paul Sartre, the intellectual superstar of existentialists.

'Hell is other people,' Julian would announce, dramatically, when I asked him why he didn't engage with anyone else. We'd argue for a while, and he'd stun me into silence with oblique explanations for his behaviour, referencing this or that philosopher, and I would feel stupid, torn and unable to let go of his mystery.

In my final year, I jumped on a train to visit my parents for Easter. Dad was at work that Saturday morning, and Mum and I were sitting at the table decorating hard-boiled eggs for Easter Sunday's breakfast.

'How's Julian?' Mum asked. She'd been too polite to broach the subject when I turned up alone on Good Friday with little warning. I could feel tears gathering and my vision blurred.

'Mum,' I said in a quivering voice. 'Do you remember Joe Platt?'

She looked up from painting her egg. 'Of course, love, what a funny question.' Putting her brush down and reaching for her cigarettes, she said, 'He was a dark horse if ever there was one.'

'Do you think joining the army sorted him out like Dad insisted it would?'

'Well now, love, that was a long time ago. I don't know what became of him.'

'I do,' I said.

Lighting a menthol cigarette, she looked quizzically at me. I continued. 'I saw him working behind a bar in a gay disco.'

'A what?' Mum exclaimed, her eyes widening as blue smoke plumed from her lips.

'Julian took me to one.'

'Did he now?'

'Yes.' I paused. 'He'd said he wanted to tell me something. And it was my birthday, so I thought...'

'I see.' Mum's gaze was steady as she nodded her head slowly to the beat of something ancient.

'Julian,' I said, 'he's like Joe Platt.'

'Like Joe,' she repeated mechanically. After a short silence, she continued, 'but I thought you two might get married.'

'So did I.' The tears flowed freely down my cheeks.

'He made a cracking lasagne,' she said and shook her head. Then, in her soft Southern Irish accent, ' Well they do say, there's nowt so queer as folk.'

'Mum!'

I laughed and she did, too. Suddenly, I felt so much better.

When I think of that childhood summer of 1966, I can almost feel the cold crackle of the frozen cream soda on my tongue and hear my mother's comical way of speaking. I miss her more and more as each year passes, and now understand how she lightened the load in uncertain times.

THE LIGHTHOUSE

I watch her throw her green gown over everything, buoyed by the warm breeze, and they see that the wait is over. Her febrile tendrils float, interweave, settle and seed. As she waves her delicate fingers over things, they burst to life. Everyone loves her. She brings the light. Curtains pull back and she dances into the room, circles to scatter the dust motes that twinkle in the air. She wafts through the laundry on the line to saturate it with the crisp aroma of spring. Young children fall fast asleep on their feathery pillows, sucking in the tiny molecules of the earth in bloom. She is the favourite. But I can no longer loiter or accept my status. When it's my turn, they start grumbling. To them, I am barren ground. But I am not that. Don't I scatter my diamond-speckled petticoats over the land? Create intricate spirals on leaves and windows? I crisp up the yellow lichen to shine in the weak sun. Stop waterfalls in mid-flow to suspend them in the frosty air. They shimmer and refract the fading light, sometimes a plummy dark red stretching over an inky sky. Shall we take a look at those who don't enjoy my talents?

'Ella, hurry!' said Jamie.

'I'm almost ready, just not sure what to pack,' Ella called down from their bedroom. Jamie took the stairs two at a time. He planned to arrive before dusk to witness it descend. He tripped on the last step and steadied himself on the wall.

'It's not a working lighthouse,' Jamie said, as he riffled through Ella's suitcase. 'I'd suggest summer stuff with a couple of jumpers thrown in.'

'Walking boots?'

'Yep, the guidebook insists.'

Half an hour later, Ella and Jamie joined the A55 Expressway to Llandudno. Ella drove fast. The countryside flew by, a film of shapes and shades of green spotted with sheep and bordered by swathes of blinding yellow rapeseed.

'How many apartments are there?' Ella asked.

'Three, but we have the best.' Jamie flung his arm out of the window, trailing it in the cooling air.

'How so?'

'I booked the Lamp Room Suite, where the Optic used to be.'

Ella let out a squeal. 'I love you, Jamie boy.'

They drove through the seaside resort and up the hill of Marine Drive, past the glittering gates of the country estate that stretched to the sea. The lighthouse stood at the edge of a curved promontory, beneath which sheer cliffs dropped to the crashing ocean.

After guest registration at the cottage, the couple picked their way to the lighthouse down a curved, uneven path. Jamie unlocked the oak door to the Lamp Room and pushed it back. 'Oh, my freaking God,' he said.

The room swam in a dazzle of light. A floor-to-ceiling glass window gave a 280-degree panoramic view of the sea and rugged cliffs to one side. The mighty Optic that was once the centre of the room, signalling to seafarers the dangers of the rocky shores beneath, had now gone. Ella rushed to the bed and fell on it. 'It's unreal,' she laughed. 'Pinch me, Jamie.' She rolled over on the four-poster, kicking her legs in the air. The Victorian décor recreated the style of the year the lighthouse opened, adorned with suffocating materials and chunky furniture.

'Is there Wi-Fi?' Ella asked.

'Who needs it?' Jamie said, over his shoulder, while he pulled parcels from the hamper and arranged them on a table. The champagne cork shot across the room and Jamie toasted his choice of a weekend. Glasses chinked, and they snuggled into a sumptuous rosewood settee in anticipation of seeing the daylight dissolve. Jamie had rehearsed his question to Ella.

Oh, the lovers of summer who watch the sun sink below the horizon, never thinking their love could follow. I will give them an out-of-season gift to shake their faith in my rival.

'I wish we could open the windows. The room stinks of salmon,' said Ella.

Jamie leaned over and kissed Ella on her bloomy cheek. 'Never satisfied, my darling,' he said. They gazed out to sea, heads light with champagne. His heart fluttered.

'What's that dark smudge on the left?' Ella asked.

Jamie sat up and peered out. 'Dunno!'

Ella grabbed the courtesy binoculars from the table, stood up and skipped to the windows. Jamie leaned to pour himself another drink. 'We might have to call room service,' he said as he waggled the empty bottle. 'We're out of champers.'

'It's getting bigger, and it's moving this way,' Ella said.

'Do you think it's a storm?' Jamie asked.

He patted the settee. 'I checked the forecast, and no precipitation was mentioned. Come back here.'

'Let's go out for a walk.' Ella grabbed Jamie's hand and yanked him up.

'But we've just settled in,' he said. Ella threw his jacket at him. 'Come on, before the sun sets.'

Standing at the edge of the promontory, they stared at the darkening sky.

'Maybe we should go back now?' Jamie suggested. Suddenly, a gust of wind tugged them around and shunted them forward. Halfway back to the lighthouse, a booming crack flashed across the sky. Coconut sized hailstones pelted down, crashing into the sea and smashing on the rocks in a frenzy of white. Ella screamed and grabbed Jamie's hand to steady herself from the force of the wind. Jamie pitched forward, and they fell to the ground, their fingers plunged into a blanket of freezing hail. The wind gusted at seventy miles an hour, and they could no longer stand upright. The couple crunched and slithered on all fours along the ground back to the lighthouse.

Now, they should question the so-called advantage of August.

'Jesus, Jamie, what's happening?' Ella said, rubbing her soaked hair with a towel. Jamie flicked on the TV, searching for a news or weather channel.

'I don't know, babes. Fingers crossed, we can still windsurf tomorrow.'

Ah, such faith. I think not.

After hot showers, they climbed into bed, made lazy love, and fell asleep. Ella was the first to wake up to the rumbling in the wall behind the bedposts. She shook Jamie awake.

'What does an earthquake feel like?' Ella asked as the chandelier rattled and swung.

'It's a storm, that's all, you drama queen.' Jamie reached out for Ella, freezing air goose-pimpled his arm, his breath puffed white in the gloom.

'What the...'

A towering wave lashed the windows before surging back in a slick. The panes rattled. Ella gripped the duvet to her chest as a boom shook the floor. Dark, foaming waves smashed into the windows, one after another, rising and falling against the shivering glass. The panels buckled. One snapped with a deafening crack. Shattered glass flew everywhere. Freezing seawater burst through. Ella screamed. The sea gushed inside in a torrent.

Her green skirts rustle as she moves towards me, warm breath in my ear.

'Don't covet what you have not,' she implores. 'You have your place. Many love you for providing resting time and for the beautiful silence that settles over the sleeping earth. For the low light that sifts through stark branches in the forest. For the cut diamond winking of night stars and the nestling buds beneath that are slowly moving up towards my light. But save them,' she begs. And I rush my storm away. I watch them sitting, soaking on the floor, laughing as the dawn breaks.

CEDRIC'S CHRISTMAS

Cedric trudged along the snowy street. 'I'm so lonely,' he said out loud, but passers-by ignored him. It was Christmas Eve, and all Cedric wished for was a friend to share the holidays with. Cedric had been friendless for quite some time and had become slightly eccentric. *No one cares about me, so I can do as I please*, he reasoned to himself as he pulled items out of cupboards and watched them smash on the floor. Earlier that day, he'd sat next to an older gentleman on a bus. 'Hello,' Cedric said, but the man continued to fiddle with his phone. Cedric could see he had forgotten how to access his contacts, so he reached over and tapped the man's phone to help. But the man did not say 'thank you', he just continued to call his wife to tell her to defrost the turkey. This sort of rude behaviour infuriated Cedric, so he pulled the man's jacket as he got up from his seat and the man stumbled back down, a little surprised.

Cedric was forgetful himself, and there had been something nagging him all day. He stayed on the bus for the return journey to the little market town to fill his time. It was warm, the windows steamed with condensation, and the general fogginess comforted him, reminding him of the journeys he and his wife, Agatha, had taken so many times to the Christmas market.

Back in town, Cedric alighted the bus. He shuffled to the market's centre, where a children's choir sang 'In the Bleak Midwinter' beneath the Christmas tree. He stood amongst the crowd, observing people's breaths streaming out as they chatted and smiled at one another. 'I wish someone would smile at me,' Cedric said out loud, but nobody responded. He left the square to walk along the snowy side streets lined with townhouses. He became aware of a white terrier trotting along beside him, glancing up at him now and then in anticipation. Cedric bent to pat him. He wagged his tail, leapt in little circles and then ran ahead. Cedric followed. After turning a corner, dashing through the churchyard, scampering through the lych-gate, the dog came to rest at the side of a grave. The night sky, pinpricked with stars and a full moon, shone on the frosted grass peeping through the snow. The dog sat, wagging his tail, swishing the snow aside. When Cedric caught up, he leaned to pat him and was surprised his head was so cold. Cedric tried to read the inscription where the dog sat sentinel, but the moonshine was not bright enough for his aged eyes. He reached into his pocket, pulled out his petrol lighter, flicked it open, and ignited the blue flame. He held the light close to the stone and read it. 'Ah, I remember now,' he said to the dog, settled on the ground, which looked up at him with the widest eyes.

'Here lies Cedric Merryman and his faithful friend, Snowball, who left this earth on 24th of December 1996.'

THE SUITCASE OF SECRETS

Warsaw, 1940

Roman

Roman leapt from the tram as it swayed along its tracks in the freezing evening air. His boots hit the snow with a thud. He skidded to a halt at the sales kiosk, where people shuffled in a queue for their newspapers. Their white breaths billowed. Roman winked at the pretty young girl inside, who flushed and smiled. He laughed, performed a little jump, and then ran to the heavy doors of his family's apartment block. Roman had recently discovered what being handsome meant but did not dwell on it. Inside the building, he bounded two steps at a time to their first-floor apartment to thump on the door.

Footsteps clicked from inside, and his older sister, Elouna, swung it open and grinned.

'Roman, you're late home,' she said, and waved a mocking finger.

They scampered down the parquet hallway into the drawing room, where the fire glinted off the Christmas decorations. The air was filled with the sharp aroma of pine.

'I went to see Noam's family, but his neighbours said they've moved to the Old Town.'

Elouna turned to Roman. 'Papa said you shouldn't go there anymore. It's not safe.'

'I know, but I miss him at school.'

Elouna ruffled Roman's thick hair and chuckled.

'Come on, little one. Let's play a game of chess. See if you've learned enough to beat your older sister.'

'Don't call me "little one"! I'm fourteen now and nearly as tall as you.'

'Sorry, it just slipped out.'

After flinging his satchel into his room, Roman slipped into a chair by the window, pulled one curtain open, and gazed into the street below. His father warned they should shut the curtains when the afternoon light died, but Roman adored watching the trundling trams and busy people hurrying around the city. Elouna set out the wooden chessboard on a table and commanded Roman to consider his first move. While he concentrated, she stood up to shut the green brocade curtain again.

'We don't want Papa to worry,' she said as she slid back down into her chair.

'Where's Mama?' Roman asked as his hand hovered over the carved chess pieces. He hoped to guess Elouna's reaction to provide a clue to his intended move.

'I'm not sure. Maybe still at school. But Mama said nothing about a teacher meeting tonight.'

Roman looked up from the chessboard when he heard a key in the front door lock. By the clipped footsteps in the hallway, he knew it was their father rather than their mother. When the drawing room door opened, a rush of cold air swept in with Ludwig, their father, whose face looked stung from the icy night air.

Elouna jumped from her seat and greeted him with a kiss on both cheeks.

'Oh! You're frozen!' she said.

'The trams are uncomfortable at this time of year.' Ludwig looked around the apartment.

'You've still got your hat on, Papa,' said Elouna.

Ludwig reached up and patted his fur hat. 'So, I have.'

He removed it and scratched his scalp.

'Where is your mama?' he asked.

'We don't know. She's not home yet,' Elouna said.

Roman saw a flash of worry flit across his father's face.

'Well, I'm sure there's a perfect reason. Maybe a school meeting she forgot to mention?' Elouna nudged her father towards the crackling fire, where he stood and rubbed his hands together, light steam rising from his snow-dampened trousers.

'Are you hungry, my children?'

'Yes, a little, but we can wait.' Elouna glanced at Roman. 'Can't we?'

He nodded, although his stomach rumbled.

'Well, that's just as well as it's time for the broadcast,' Ludwig said. 'Sit with me.'

The three settled around the walnut-clad wireless to one side of the fireplace, where leaping flames licked the chimney's throat. Ludwig eased into a leather Chesterfield that groaned as he sank. Roman and Elouna perched on a green velvet sofa opposite.

'As always, I will remind you not to let anyone, friends or relatives, know we listen to the BBC Overseas Service because..?' He stared directly at Elouna to finish his sentence.

'Listening to outside broadcasts is forbidden. It's a punishable offence under the Third Reich,' she said, solemnly looking at Roman.

He nodded. Roman knew they must obey this frightening rule. Ludwig turned the dial, and the wireless slowly hummed into life. Roman thought its pewter grill resembled a human face, the eyes and mouth illuminated from the filament inside. To him, it looked curiously sad.

Roman listened to the radio, but his attention strayed to footsteps that sounded outside their apartment. Ludwig leaned forward and snapped off the radio. He pressed a finger to his lips. All three held their breaths until the footsteps receded down the hallway. When it was silent, Ludwig switched the set back on. The announcer reported that an RAF raid on Mannheim, Germany, had been successful. It was retaliation for a series of devastating air attacks by the Germans the previous month over Bristol, Liverpool, and Southampton, which left those major British cities burned out and ruined. They had savagely bombed Warsaw at the beginning of the invasion. Roman recalled the terror of those times, darting between blazing, falling masonry, to get home and seeing people dying or lying helpless in the streets.

Ludwig clicked the radio off when the broadcast ended, and all three sat in silence. Roman's fingertip traced crumbs in the crevice between the sofa seats from when he and his mother had eaten toasted rye bread the previous evening. His stomach lurched.

'Your mother is very late,' Ludwig said as he glanced at the mahogany clock on the mantelpiece that struck seven. He stood up and pulled at the bottom of his suit jacket. Their phone shrilled in the hallway. 'Ah!' said Ludwig. 'News, perhaps.' He hurried to the phone. Roman and Elouna followed him to hang inside the oak door frame.

'Ludwig Kozynski speaking.'

Roman watched his father, who clung to the receiver with both hands as he turned his back to them.

'Are you sure?' Ludwig said. He listened some more.

'Yes, yes, I understand.' He leaned one arm on the wall behind the telephone table to steady himself while a muffled voice filtered from the receiver.

Elouna threw her arm around Roman's shoulders. He grasped her wrist. It was warm and, momentarily, comforting to him.

'There's just one problem.' Ludwig turned briefly towards his children. 'My wife isn't home yet.'

As more inaudible conversation followed, Roman's throat tightened. His father gently placed the receiver in its cradle and stood motionless for a moment, as though lost in a dream. He shook his head and clapped his hands together.

'Okay, children, we must go away for a few days. Let's pack.'

'What?' said Elouna.

Roman stood motionless, trying to comprehend.

Ludwig hurried them back into the centre of the drawing room. He placed a hand on each of their shoulders and leaned in, conspiratorially.

'A friend needs help. We must visit him.' He nodded at them with a strained smile. 'So, off you both go to pack, immediately.'

'Where are we going?' Elouna asked.

'Don't ask questions. Just do as I say. We leave tonight.'

'We can't just leave. What about Mama?' Roman stood his ground against the gentle push of his father's hand.

'She'll meet us there. Now, get to it as quickly as possible.'

Elouna pushed Roman into his bedroom. 'I'll help you pack.'

She stretched up to grab his suitcase from the top of the wardrobe, pulled it clear, and threw it on the bed. The latches sprang open and a layer of grey dust flew from the lid. She yanked open the wardrobe drawers and grabbed two red woollen jumpers.

'Here,' she said as she bundled them onto Roman's bed, 'pack these.'

Roman watched. His thoughts froze. His knees buckled. Everything was happening too quickly for him to think clearly.

'Get your boots and socks,' said Elouna.

Hit by the urgency, Roman snapped from his confusion and grabbed clothes from the drawers. He stuffed them into the suitcase with shaking hands.

'I'm okay,' he said. 'I can do it. You pack your things, Elouna.'

Roman's heart raced as she hurried from his room. The sound of heavy footsteps, which thumped from downstairs, diverted his attention. Roman stopped what he was doing and crept into the hall, where he saw Ludwig huddled with Elouna. He ran to join them. The sound of approaching footsteps grew louder, and violent banging began on their apartment door. His father raised a finger in the air and motioned for Roman to listen.

'Quick!' Ludwig whispered to them. 'Go to Roman's room and lock yourselves in. Do not come out until I say.'

Elouna darted towards Roman's room. He scrambled after her, skidding on the newly polished parquet floor. They sheltered, breathless, behind his bedroom door with their ears pressed against it.

'Open up! Open up!' a voice bellowed outside their apartment, accompanied by even louder banging at their front door.

Roman could hear his father rushing around the apartment while the banging continued.

'You must open, now!' a man's voice roared.

Roman heard what sounded like repeated kicking. He whispered to Elouna to step back a little as he peeped out. His father stood behind the front door, straightening his jacket, while the wood shuddered from the blows delivered by whoever was outside. Finally, Ludwig smoothed his hair and slowly opened the door.

The Gestapo officers rushed in.

Roman silently closed his bedroom door and told Elouna not to make a sound.

'Ludwig Kozynski?' a voice bawled.

'Yes, that's me.'

'Where's the rest of your family?'

Roman heard his father say they were visiting relatives out of town, and the thump of an assault followed.

'Men, search the apartment.'

Roman tiptoed to his bedroom window with Elouna in tow. Her warm hand had turned cold.

'You escape through here,' he whispered as he eased the window up as quietly as possible. Roman prayed the mechanism would not stick, as it often did. He needed it to open wide enough for Elouna to squeeze out. The window slowly yielded to his effort. The icy night air smacked him as he helped Elouna clamber over the window ledge to dangle her feet outside.

Elouna grabbed his hand and turned to him. He looked down to see a military truck parked beneath. It appeared empty.

'I can't!' she said, glancing into the snowy street in terror.

'You must. It's the only way. Jump, and roll when you hit the ground.' Roman briefly kissed her cheek. 'I'll follow you,' he said.

They stared at each other, momentarily. Roman's heart seemed to thump at the base of his gullet. Elouna slid from the icicle-covered ledge. Her skirt billowed as she plunged into the deep snow with a thud. Roman saw her lying there for a few seconds, stunned. Elouna scrambled to her feet, brushed herself down, and sneaked off into the night without a coat but at least with boots. Roman pulled the window shut and turned towards his half-packed suitcase. His door flew open, and a Gestapo guard rushed in with his rifle at full tilt.

'Stop!'

Roman raised his hands as he had seen people do in the streets of the Old Town, where Jewish families were now forced to live. The guard glanced around the room and yanked the wardrobe open. Satisfied there was no one there, he turned to Roman.

'Out! Out!' He butted Roman in the stomach with his rifle.

As Roman staggered into the hallway, he saw his father standing with his hands on his head. Blood trickled from one corner of his mouth while a guard trained a rifle at his temple. Another ransacked their drawing room. He kicked aside the chairs at the table and smashed the chessboard with the rifle butt.

Anya

Earlier that day, across town, Anya Kozynska watched over her primary school pupils who scrambled into their boots, coats, and hats for the freezing journey home. She loved that time of day because the children looked happy and excited as they jumped up to pull their clothing from the brightly coloured wall hooks. Anya's gaze halted at the sight of Irena perched on the bench beneath the coats, struggling to lace up her clumsy-looking boots, far too large for such a small girl.

Anya approached her and bent down. 'Do you need some help, Irena?'

Irena raised her head, her heart-shaped face flushed with embarrassment.

'No, Miss Kozynska.' She tugged the lace at the top of one boot to tighten it. 'These were my brother's, before me. My mama says they have life left in them.'

'Indeed!'

Anya ran her hand over the toe of the boot and felt a lump at its tip.

'Let's just see what's happening here, shall we?' She slid her hands to the top, smiling.

Anya knew Irena's father died during the outbreak of the invasion, and her mother struggled to keep the family of three boys and two girls fed and clothed. Anya untied the laces, slipped the boot off, and probed inside. Her fingers prodded what felt like a wedge of damp paper at the toe. It had scrunched up to one side, causing Irena's foot to slide around when she walked.

'Well, I can fix this for you.'

Anya watched Irena stare at her thin knees. 'Thank you, Miss Kozynska.'

As Anya redistributed the padding, careful not to pull it out and embarrass Irena further, she said, 'You know, I have some boots at home which belonged to my daughter, Elouna. She grew out of them a long time ago. I'm sure they're your size. Shall I bring them for you tomorrow?'

Irena's eyes widened. 'But Mama might be cross with me.'

As she secured Irena's laces, Anya said, 'I will write her a note to go with the shoes. What do you say?'

Irena smiled and slid from her seat.

'Come on, follow me.'

Anya walked the little girl to the outside door. She watched Irena clump through the thick snow, and her heart felt heavy for the girl's future.

Anya pushed the door closed against the drifting snow and turned to see Mr Krause, the headteacher, striding towards her.

'Miss Kozynska, do you have a moment?'

'Why, yes, Mr Krause, of course.'

Krause's small eyes flashed behind his steel-rimmed glasses. Anya had recently noticed him studying her intently as she went about the work she loved, but stifled her feelings of unease. He had never acted unprofessionally towards her, but she could not relax in his company. She and her family recently attended the school's Christmas party, where Ludwig and Krause spoke of business matters and the political situation. She avoided Krause and chatted with the other teachers. Afterwards, at home, she sought Ludwig's opinion of him.

'Hard to pin down,' he'd said.

Krause filled her with a sense of discomfort.

'Follow me.' He crooked a finger and hurried to his office. 'Sit down,' he said as he hovered nearby, arms folded over his skinny chest. 'Can you stay longer to assist me in checking the school finances tonight? I have a report to prepare for tomorrow morning for the school board.'

'Well, I...' Anya looked him directly in the eye. She saw Krause's pursed lips and arms tighten across his jacket. 'Of course, Mr Krause.'

'Excellent! I expected you would be at home with finances.'

Anya stared at him but said nothing as she sat down to attend to the ledger on Krause's desk. She wasn't sure exactly what he was implying.

'Your husband's a businessman. Or, am I mistaken?' Krause said, his head cocked to one side.

Anya adjusted her hair and breathed deeply. 'Yes, he is. So, what exactly am I required to do?'

Krause closed his office curtains and turned to her. 'Find evidence the bursar is stealing from me. I suspect he's Jewish, though he hides it.'

Elouna

Her jump from the window shocked Elouna. But, with every sense on high alert, she glanced around. Curfew had started, and the street was empty. The desolation and silence of the night struck her as eerie. It was the first time she had broken the curfew restrictions, which was extremely frightening. She knew anyone caught would be arrested. Some were immediately shot. Elouna needed to find somewhere to hide quickly. She set off towards a nearby park. Thankfully, the deep snow muffled her footsteps. As she ran, she was aware of semi-crouching to diminish her outline. Her rapid breaths steamed white into the night air around her head. As the park came into view, a spurt of energy added momentum to her rush. Thick, evergreen bushes enclosed it. She slowed and headed to the densest section, squatting. As her breath steadied, Elouna noticed the sounds of a commotion that clattered through the still night. A shot cracked. Someone barked orders that echoed in the emptiness of the streets. Her stomach knotted because she guessed it was concerning her father and brother.

The cold stung Elouna's hands. She glanced down to see them plunged deep in the snow to steady her position, a posture she had taken, unaware. A vision of her coat and gloves on her bed flashed before her. Suddenly, an engine caught as it ignited, and the rumble of a truck sounded over the cobblestones. The vehicle roared past the bushes, its headlights flashing through winter shrubbery. Elouna held her breath as fear prickled her scalp. She yanked her hands from the snow and tucked them under her armpits for warmth. She stretched shakily from her hunched position and slunk off towards the school where she prayed her mother was.

When she arrived at the school, her whole body trembled from shock. It was impossible to process. The school was in darkness, apart from one place where a dim light shone behind a curtained window. Elouna knew it was the headmaster's quarters from the Christmas party when Mr Krause had shown her and Roman around, insisting his tree was the tallest in all of Warsaw's homes.

She crept past the window and around to the rear of the building. Her eyes had adjusted to the gloom, and she spotted a small open window. Elouna searched everywhere and found a litter bin tall enough to stand on to reach the ledge. She dragged it to the wall with as little noise as possible and clambered on top. The window opened into the school kitchen, and directly beneath was a draining board stacked with pots and pans. Elouna pulled the window open, and to her relief, the gap was wide enough to squeeze her slender body through in a crab-like manoeuvre. She slid down and planted a foot and hand between a skillet and a boiling pan. Her foot caught a pan that crashed to the floor. A brief silence followed where she held her breath and cursed in her head.

Someone yelled out, 'Who's there?'

Footsteps thundered outside. The kitchen door creaked open to a beam of light, carried by the headmaster, Mr Krause, that swung around the room.

'It's me, Elouna Kozynska, Anya's daughter.'

He snapped on the light. 'What the devil?'

The brightness dazzled her. Despite that, Elouna completed her descent and jumped down.

'Help me, Mr Krause. Please,' she said as her knees buckled from the events of that night, and without warning, she crumpled to the stone-flagged floor before she lost consciousness.

When Elouna came round, Mr Krause said, 'Can you hear me?'

'Yes.'

She tried to sit upright but was dizzy and remembered not eating since breakfast.

'Let me help.' Krause hooked his hands under her armpits and pulled Elouna to stand. 'Are you hurt?'

'No.'

He led her to the cook's table and eased her into a chair. 'You're alright now, Miss Kozynska.'

Krause eyed her damp clothes. Elouna felt as though she hovered above herself and watched. Nothing seemed real anymore. A short while ago, she and Roman played chess safely in their home before a knock on the door ripped their life apart. Elouna did not know why the Gestapo invaded their home or what happened to Roman and her father. And her mother was missing, too.

She cried.

Krause crossed the kitchen and drew the blinds down. 'I'll make some tea, and you tell me what's happened,' he said.

He shuffled to the stove to prepare their drink. The red flame leapt to life as Krause lit the gas with a smooth taper. He jumped back. Elouna tried to compose her thoughts to relay the evening events to Krause, but an idea darted through her mind.

'Mr Krause, what time did my mother leave school tonight?'

Krause turned slowly from the stove. 'Why, my dear?'

'It's just, she hadn't arrived home before…'

He folded his arms. 'Before what?' Krause stared at her so hard she felt herself recoil from his gaze. 'Your mother left a little later than usual, but I can't imagine why she hasn't yet returned. Perhaps you're mistaken?'

Elouna's heart thumped at the base of her throat. She needed to tell someone what happened, or she would burst. Krause was her mother's employer, after all. She should trust him.

'We…' She hesitated, picturing the scene in her mind, and decided to tell him about the forbidden radio broadcast wasn't safe. 'Some German soldiers burst into our home tonight. I think they took Papa and Roman away.'

Krause uncrossed his arms and rested his knuckles on his hips. 'Why?'

'I don't know. I escaped.'

'But why would they arrest your father?'

Elouna tried to catch the expression in his eyes, but the heat misted his glasses.

A silence followed.

'These are indeed strange times,' Krause said as the kettle's shrill whistle sliced the air.

He poured the boiled water into a teapot and clamped the billowing steam beneath the cracked lid.

'I must find Mama.'

'I'm afraid you can't do anything now. It's curfew.' Krause returned to the table with their drinks. He set them down but remained standing. 'When you've had your tea, get some rest. Whatever has happened has given you a terrible fright.' Krause smiled and laid a hand on Elouna's shoulder. 'Tomorrow morning, I'm sure your mother will be in school, and everything will be fine.'

A grey fog cleared momentarily for Elouna, and a lump gathered in her throat. 'Do you think so?'

'I'm sure.' Cogs turned behind his eyes. 'I tell you what, you can take your tea, and I'll put you in the children's sickbay to sleep. There's a bed and a washbasin.'

She followed him down the cold corridor to a door he had to unlock. Krause motioned for Elouna to go inside, and he flicked on a dingy light.

'It's more comfortable than it looks,' he said, pointing to a tiny bed. 'I'll see you in the morning. Goodnight.'

Elouna collapsed onto the bed and curled into a foetal position on the scratchy grey covers, too tired to climb inside. She scanned the room. A bright poster featured smiling boys with blond hair and blue eyes. It invited them to hike in the mountains with the Hitler Youth movement.

Thank you for reading an extract from *The Suitcase of Secrets*, first published in 2023, Copyright of Julie Fearn. I hope you enjoyed it - the full novel is available from Amazon in Kindle and paperback.

If you'd like to keep in touch with me, please sign up for my author updates at juliefearn.com

About the novel, The Suitcase of Secrets

As the daughter of Polish and Irish immigrants, Julie weaves elements of her family's lived experience with meticulously researched history in a heartfelt debut novel. The book centres around Roman, a Polish refugee settling in West Yorkshire in the 1940s, and the tragedy of displacement following WW2. While creating a life for himself, he finds love - but the horrors of war refuse to stay buried. Can he heal, or will the ghosts of war leave his new life in ruin?

ABOUT JULIE FEARN

Julie studied creative writing at postgraduate level at York University, where her short story, The Baba Yaga Tree, was published in their anthology. She was one of six Yorkshire authors picked by Kemps Bookshop in Malton to be promoted in 2023, and returned to Kemps to discuss her novel and the background in 2024.

Her author events include speaking at Barnsley Council's Holocaust Memorial Day, the WI, U3A events, Harrogate Library's Books & Beverages and presenting her work with the group Promoting Yorkshire Authors in Knaresborough for the FEVA Festival. She has spoken on BBC Radio York, Jorvik Radio and Bradford Community Broadcasting about her novel *The Suitcase of Secrets*.

Julie is currently working on her second novel, a departure from *The Suitcase of Secrets* as a women's fiction thriller. She's a lifelong lover of stories and believes the narrative drive is hardwired in us all. In her fantasy life, she sits by an open fire at night with others, listening to and telling stories while the wolves howl in the background. To find out more and keep in touch with Julie, you can join her author's update list at juliefearn.com

Printed in Great Britain
by Amazon